PATCH
A Baby Mink

The mink family's den was a warm little room under the roots of a big tree. Patch was the smallest of the family. He was always at the bottom when the mink babies bundled to-gether to keep warm.

This is the story of how Patch and his sisters and brothers grew up. It is the story of their first lessons in the school of the woods. And it is the story of a boy and a girl who became just a little wiser through their first meeting with the mink family.

A SEE AND READ

Beginning to Read Book

PATCH

A Baby Mink

by Virginia Frances Voight

Illustrated by Steele Savage

G. P. Putnam's Sons   New York

Also by Virginia Frances Voight:

PICTA THE PAINTED TURTLE

NATHAN HALE

Text © 1965 by Virginia Frances Voight
Illustrations © 1965 by Steele Savage
Library of Congress Catalog Card Number: 65-13301
All rights reserved
MANUFACTURED IN THE UNITED STATES OF AMERICA
Published simultaneously in the Dominion of Canada
by Longmans Canada Limited, Toronto
06208
Third Impression

The mink family lived on the bank of a woodland pond. Their den was a warm little room under the roots of a big tree. In front of the den a little beach led down to the water.

Inside the den, six baby minks were
sleeping on a bed of pine needles.
Patch was the smallest of the family.

He was always at the bottom when
the babies bundled together to keep
warm. He had been no bigger than a
peanut when he was born. Even now,
his eyes were still shut and he had
hardly any fur at all.

Patch cuddled against his soft-furred mother to drink her good milk. He made a purring sound when Mother washed him. He drank milk and he took naps all day long. Every day he grew a little bigger. His coat grew in soft and fluffy. It was a lovely golden-brown color.

One day Patch found that his eyes
were open.

Until now he had smelled his
mother and touched her. Now he
could see her as well! Best of all, he
could see a sunbeam peeping in at
the door of the den.

9

Patch wanted to touch the sun-beam and smell it, as he smelled everything he found. He crawled to the door on his short legs. But his mother took him by the ear with her teeth and pulled him back.

The mink kittens were still too little to go outdoors.

Now that their eyes were open, the little minks played all day in the den. They chased their fluffy tails. They jumped on one another, and sometimes they bit and cuffed. Because Patch was the smallest, the others rolled him about. But he was always ready for another game.

One summer morning Mother Mink
went outside and called to the babies
to follow her. Patch was the first kitten to leave the dark den. He stood
on the beach, blinking his eyes in
wonder.

He had thought that the mink den
was the whole world. Now he saw
the blue pond and the pine trees,
tall and green.

He saw a dark furry animal who looked like Mother Mink but was bigger.

This was Father Mink.

Most of the year Father Mink lived
by himself. But in summer he stayed
with his family, helping Mother find
food for the babies. Now he would
help teach the kittens lessons that all
wild animals need to know.

Linda and Ted had come to spend
the summer at the pond. Early on
their first morning they walked down
to the water.

Squirrels were playing in the
branches overhead. A chipmunk
peeped at the children from beneath
a root. A rabbit hopped away to hide.

Father Mink was running along the beach, carrying a fish.

"Ted, look!" Linda cried. "What kind of animal is that?"

"I guess it's a mink," said Ted.

Father Mink took off into the woods in big jumps. He was so long, and his legs were so short, that he humped up when he ran.

Linda laughed. "He looks like a big inchworm."

"No worm ever ran as fast as that," her brother said.

Soon Father Mink was lost among the trees.

"I hope we see him again someday," said Ted.

It was fun to know that a wild mink lived near them.

The mink kittens were playing
under the den tree when Father Mink
came home. He dropped the fish in
front of them. Until now the babies
had lived on milk. Now the time had
come when they must have other
food.

The kittens looked at the fish in wonder. It smelled good, but what should they do with it? Father Mink growled, as if to say, "Eat it!"

Patch pushed at the fish, then he
took a bite. Mm. It was good! He
squeaked happily. At that one of the

other kittens took a bite too. Soon all
the baby minks were eating. Their
table manners were not at all pretty.

They snapped and pulled the fish about. They pushed one another as each one tried to get the finest bits for himself.

One kitten carried a bit of fish out from under the tree.

Mother Mink gave a warning cry which meant "Come back!"

She wanted the kitten to stay under the branches, where she would be safe.

The little mink went on eating her fish. She had forgotten her very first lesson. A baby animal must come fast when its mother calls!

Then it happened. A big hawk, fly-
ing in the blue sky, saw the kitten on
the beach. He flew down and caught
her. Mother Mink ran to help her
baby, but the hawk was too fast for
her. He carried the mink kitten off to
his nest in the woods.

Mother Mink ran back and pushed the other kittens into the den. Patch moved too slowly, so she caught him with her teeth and carried him.

The five babies who were left had
to stay inside the rest of the day.
Mother Mink sat growling by the
door. She was warning her babies of
the danger in the woods and under
the open sky.

That night the cry of a big owl sounded in the woods.

HOO HOO HOO

In the mink den Mother Mink growled.

"The owl would like to catch a mink for his supper," she was saying.

In the woods a red fox barked.

Mother Mink snarled. She was telling her babies,

"Watch out for foxes! They eat baby minks."

And so the mink kittens had their lessons in the school of the woods.

Every day the little minks played
by the water while Mother stayed
near.

They chased hoptoads, and they
chased each other along the beach.

They fished for tadpoles and little fish.
Once a baby mouse ran out of the
woods. Patch tried to catch it, but the
little mouse ran hard and got away.

Fish was the food that the mink
family liked best of all. Father and
Mother Mink went fishing every day.
They could swim underwater as well
as any fish. But the baby minks had
to have swimming lessons, just like
girls and boys.

At first they just ducked and splashed and swam near the beach. Mother Mink tried to get them to swim far out. Often she would take one of them for a ride on her back up the pond.

Once, when Linda and Ted were
in their boat, they saw an animal
swimming nearby.

"It's the mink," Ted cried.

Linda blinked and looked again.
"Oh, Ted, there's a little mink riding
on the big one's back!"

The little mink was Patch. His mother was taking him for a ride while Father stayed with the other kittens. He was cuddled down on Mother's back, holding tight with his paws. It was easy to see that he was having lots of fun.

But now Mother Mink had seen the boat. She swam back to shore and cuffed Patch ahead of her into the woods. They ran home to the den and hid until the children went away.

After that the children looked for the minks every day. They saw them again early one morning when they were fishing from their boat. This was the morning that Mother Mink took all her babies for a swim.

The children laughed with delight when they saw the mink family. Mother Mink swam first with the kittens following one by one.

All the babies could swim quite well now. But because Patch was still the smallest, he swam last in line. His little paws were working hard as he tried to catch up with the others.

The children sat so still that Mother Mink swam right past the boat. Four little minks swam close behind her. Last of all came Patch, far behind the others.

Ted picked up his fishing net.

"I'm going to catch that little one for a pet," he said.

When Patch got to the boat, Ted swished the net into the water.

"I've got him!" he cried.

He pulled the net into the boat. Inside was Patch, who let out a wild cry for help.

Mother Mink turned when she heard Patch's cry. She hissed to the other kittens to wait where they were. Then she swam back to the boat.

Ted had put the net down between Linda and himself. The little mink peeped out at them. He was frightened, but he was angry too. These two funny beings had no right to take him out of the water! He snarled at the children and pawed at the net.

"We won't hurt you," said Linda.

She tried to play with Patch by putting her hand against the net. Patch growled and bit at it. Linda pulled her hand away.

"He doesn't like us at all," she told Ted.

Just then something hissed in the water. Ted looked over the side of the boat and there was Mother Mink! She climbed right up the side of the boat.

There she sat, growling at the children.

Linda moved to the far side of the seat. "Ted, she wants her baby back!"

Ted's father had told him that all animal mothers will fight for their little ones. Mother Mink looked as if she was about to start fighting with all her might. But still Ted did not want to let his wild pet go.

In the net Patch squeaked for his mother to come and get him. At that Mother Mink jumped down into the boat. She ran to the net and pulled at it with her teeth and paws. Then she turned, snarling.

"Ted!" Linda cried. "She is going to jump at you!"

Ted turned the net upside down over the side of the boat. Patch fell into the water. He called to his mother as he went under.

Mother Mink jumped into the water after Patch. Soon she came up again, holding Patch with her teeth.

Mother Mink turned her head so that Patch could climb upon her back. He cuddled down, purring.

At a call from their mother, the other mink kittens came swimming back. With Patch riding pick-a-back, The mink family started home.

"I'm glad you let the baby mink go," Linda told Ted.

Ted looked sadly after Patch. "I guess he wouldn't have been happy with us," he said.

Patch could have told Ted that he was right about that. No wild animal can be happy away from his woodland home.

Key Words

beach	pine
born	pond
catch (caught)	purr(ed) (ing)
chipmunk	roots
danger	smell(ed)
den	snarl(ed) (ing)
ear	squeak(ed)
eyes	sunbeam
foxes (fox)	teach
fur	teeth
golden	touch
hawk	tree
hoptoads(s)	wild
inchworm	wonder
lesson(s)	woodland
needle(s)	

The Author

VIRGINIA FRANCES VOIGHT's storybooks and nature tales have been delighting young readers in the United States and Europe for many years. She has published some thirteen children's books in addition to numerous stories and articles in *Boy's Life, Trails for Juniors, The American Girl,* and other periodicals for children. A lifelong student of American history, Miss Voight also maintains an active interest in the conservation of wildlife and natural resources. She makes her home in Connecticut and spends her summers in Maine, gathering material for the backgrounds of her books.

The Artist

STEELE SAVAGE spent the early years of his career studying and working in Paris, Vienna and London. Since that time he has been an illustrator for major national magazines, an advertising artist and a set and costume designer for the Broadway theater. In addition, Steele Savage has more than 70 illustrated books to his credit, including special editions of the classics. Mr. Savage makes his home in New York City.